T·H·E
TEDDY BEAR BOOK

by Jean Marzollo | *pictures by Ann Schweninger*

Dial Books for Young Readers ◦ *New York*

Published by Dial Books for Young Readers
A Division of NAL Penguin Inc.
2 Park Avenue, New York, New York 10016

Published simultaneously in Canada by
Fitzhenry & Whiteside Limited, Toronto.
Text copyright © 1989 by Jean Marzollo
Illustrations copyright © 1989 by Ann Schweninger
Printed in Hong Kong by
South China Printing Co.
First Edition
(b)
1 3 5 7 9 10 8 6 4 2

Library of Congress Cataloging in Publication Data

Marzollo, Jean.
The teddy bear book

[1. Teddy bears—Juvenile poetry. 2. Children's
poetry, American.] I. Schweninger, Ann, ill. II. Title.
PS3563.A777G7   1989   811'.54   87-24538
ISBN 0-8037-0524-7   ISBN 0-8037-0633-2 (lib. bdg.)

These poems are adaptations of songs, jump rope rhymes, ball-bouncing chants, cheers, and story poems that are passed from generation to generation and child to child in the oral tradition. Since love of teddy bears is another tradition continually passed on, it seemed natural to connect bears and rhymes. When I worked on the poems, I found that the bears added to the fun. Act out the rhymes with your favorite teddy bear and see if you agree.

Jean Marzollo

Ten Little Teddy Bears

One little, two little, three little teddy bears;
Four little, five little, six little teddy bears;
Seven little, eight little, nine little teddy bears;
Ten little teddy bear babies.

Ten little, nine little, eight little teddy bears;
Seven little, six little, five little teddy bears;
Four little, three little, two little teddy bears;
One little teddy bear baby.

Teddy Bear, Teddy Bear, Turn Around

Teddy Bear, Teddy Bear,
turn around.
Teddy Bear, Teddy Bear,
touch the ground.
Teddy Bear, Teddy Bear,
go to bed.
Teddy Bear, Teddy Bear,
rest your head.
Teddy Bear, Teddy Bear,
go to sleep.
Teddy Bear, Teddy Bear,
not a peep.

Strawberry Shortcake

Strawberry shortcake,
Huckleberry pie,
V-I-C-T-O-R-Y!
Are we with it?
Well, I guess,
Teddy bears, teddy bears,
Yes! Yes! Yes!

I Had a Little Teddy Bear

I had a little teddy bear,
his name was Tiny Tim.
I put him in the bathtub
to see if he could swim.

He drank up all the water,
he ate up all the soap.
I asked him if he liked it
and all he said was "Nope."

Eenie, Meenie

Eenie, meenie, minie, mo,
Catch a teddy bear by the toe,
If he hollers, let him go,
Eeenie, meenie, minie, mo.

Eenie, meenie, minie, moes,
Catch a teddy bear by the nose,
If he hollers, let him pay
Fifty dollars every day.

A Counting Chant

Teddy Bear, Teddy Bear
Took a trip
In a plane
And on a ship.
How many miles did he go?
Ten, twenty, thirty, forty,
Fifty, sixty, seventy, eighty, ninety,
One hundred!

Teddy Bear Rag

I can do the Teddy Bear,
I can do the kick.
I can do a somersault,
And I can do the split.

Teddy Bear, Teddy Bear

Teddy Bear, Teddy Bear,
Dressed in blue,
Here are the motions
You must do.
Stand at attention,
Stand at ease.
Bend your elbows,
Bend your knees.
Salute to the left,
Salute to the right.
Jump around
With all your might.
Now do the heel-toe.
Now do the split.
Now do the wiggle-waggle
Just like this.

Did You Ever?

Did you ever, ever, ever
In your teddy bear life
See a teddy bear dance
With his teddy bear wife?

No, I never, never, never
In my teddy bear life
Saw a teddy bear dance
With his teddy bear wife.

Summer Breezes

When summer breezes start to blow,
Teddy Bear runs oh, so slow.
When autumn leaves fall at last,
Teddy Bear runs oh, so fast!

Glory to the Mountain

Glory to the mountain,
Glory to the top,
Glory to my teddy bear,
And glory to my pop.
Glory to the seashore,
Glory to the sea,
Glory to my momma,
And glory to me.

Down by the Station

Down by the station, early in the morning,
See the little teddy bears all in a row;
See the engine driver pull the little throttle;
Chug, chug, poof, poof! Off they go.

Where's the Bear?

Where's the bear?
The bear's not home.
He went to Boston
To buy a comb.

Teddy Boo and Teddy Bear

Teddy Boo and Teddy Bear
Live across the way.
Every time they have a fight
This is what they say:
Icabocker, icabocker, icabocker boo!
Icabocker, soda cracker, phooey on you!

Teddy Bear Alarm

Teddy Bear, Teddy Bear,
Do not wait.
There's a fire
In number eight.

Bring your truck,
Bring your hose,
And wear your waterproof
Fireman clothes.

My Name Is Teddy

My name is Teddy.
Catch me if you dare.
This is my daddy.
He's a great big bear.
He took me to the zoo
And sat me on his knee,
And asked me twenty questions
Of what I'd like to see.
We went to see the tiger,
We went to see the hare,
We went to see the hippo
And the polar bear.

I Was Running Through the Park

I was running through the park,
I was running through the field,
When I met a senorita
With buckles on her heel.
She had a little teddy bear,
She had a little bee.
She put them on her fancy hat
And gave them all to me.

Down by the River

Down by the river
Where the green grass grows,
Sits a little teddy bear
A-washing out his clothes.

He sings a little teddy song
That's oh, so sweet,
I sing and click my fingers
And I tap my feet.

He gives me little cookies
That are oh, so sweet,
And I give him rubber booties
For his chubby little feet.

Bear Hunt

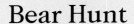

Going on a bear hunt.
I'm not afraid.
With my big trusty bag
And my lemonade.

I walk upstairs.
"Are you there?"
"No," says a voice,
"I'm not here."

Going on a bear hunt.
I'm not afraid.
With my big trusty bag
And my lemonade.

I look in the closet.
"Are you in there?"
"No," says a voice,
"I'm not here."

I look behind the bed.
"Are you there?"
"Yes!" says a voice.
"I am here!"

Teddy Bear, Rock the Chair

Teddy Bear,
Rock the chair.
Teddy Bye,
Touch the sky.
Teddy Bees,
Jump in leaves.
Teddy Bope,
Wash with soap.
Teddy Bose,
Touch your nose.
Teddy Bright,
Say good night.

Bear Light, Bear Bright

Bear light, bear bright
First bear I see tonight,
Wish I may, wish I might
Be the bear I see tonight.